DreamWorks Trolls

BIGGIE

and the Disastrous Dance

By David Lewman

Random House 🏠 New York

CHAPTER ONE

One delightfully sunny morning in Troll Village, Cooper went from pod to pod delivering invitations. Trotting along on his four feet, he sang a happy tune, bobbing his head on his long, striped neck. His yarnlike blue hair bounced under his green cap.

"I've got some mail for you! I've got some mail for me! I've got some mighty-fine mail for

every Troll I see!" he sang. *"Uh-huh! Yeah! Uh-huh! Yeah! I said MAIL!"*

Cooper arrived at Smidge's cozy little pod. Because she was the smallest adult Troll in the village, she lived in one of the smallest pods. On this lovely day, she was already outside lifting weights with her super-strong hair.

"Two hundred and six, two hundred and seven . . . ," she counted in her deep voice as she raised a heavy barbell high in the clear morning air.

"Good morning, Smidge!" Cooper called. "Got something for you, and I think you're gonna like it!"

CLUNK! Smidge set her barbell down. The impact shook the ground, sending Cooper a few inches into the air.

"Whoa!" he shouted. "That thing must weigh, like, a lot!"

"What have you got for me, Cooper?" Smidge asked eagerly. She loved surprises.

With a little bow, Cooper handed her a sparkly envelope. "An invitation!"

"Ooh!" she said, excited. "What are you inviting me to?"

Cooper looked confused. "Nothing."

Puzzled, Smidge held up the envelope. "But I thought you said this was an invitation."

"Oh, it is," Cooper said with a big toothy grin. "Definitely!"

"Then what are you inviting me to?" Smidge repeated.

"Nothing," Cooper said again, his smile disappearing.

"So . . . this is an invitation to nothing?" Smidge asked.

"Oh, no." Cooper shook his head. "It's not an invitation to nothing. It's an invitation to something."

"Oh my gah." Smidge looked even more puzzled. "I thought you said you were inviting me to nothing."

"I am," Cooper said. "I mean, I'm not inviting you to anything. But *Poppy's* inviting you to something!"

"Ohhhhh!" Smidge finally got it. "This invitation is from *Poppy*! I should have known from all the glitter." As she eagerly tore open the envelope, Cooper leaned in to get a closer look. *POOF!* Glitter shot out and landed on his nose and cheeks.

"AH-CHOO!" Cooper let out a big sneeze.

A tiny drawing of Smidge popped out of the envelope, and a sweet little voice sang, *"Smidge, you're invited!"*

"'You are hereby invited to the village square to hear a very special announcement!'" Smidge read.

"Ooh, an announcement!" Cooper echoed. "When is this announcement?"

"Let's see," Smidge said. "'Casual attire . . . come as you are . . . snacks will be provided . . .' Here it is: 'this morning'!"

Cooper looked shocked. "But it's already this morning! It's been this morning all morning!" He twisted his head around to look at the bag slung on his back. It was full of glittering invitations. "How am I going to get all these invitations delivered in time for the announcement? I'd better hurry! Zip-zippity-zip!"

Cooper tried to run off, but he was in such a rush that he got his legs all tangled up and fell to the ground. Smidge untangled his legs and helped him to his feet.

"I've got an idea!" she said. "I think I can help you get the word out about Poppy's announcement!"

"How?" Cooper asked.

"Like this!" Smidge answered. She took a deep breath, cupped her hands around her mouth, and bellowed in her deep voice, "ATTENTION, ALL TROLLS! THERE WILL BE AN IMPORTANT ANNOUNCEMENT AT THE VILLAGE SQUARE IN TWO MINUTES! BE THERE OR BE HAIRLESS!"

Smidge's powerful voice carried to the far edges of the village. Everyone heard her! The Trolls popped out of their pods, whipped their hair around branches, and zoomed through the village to the square.

Poppy was already there waiting for them.

"Good morning, everyone!" she called cheerfully from the edge of the big stage.

"Good morning, Queen Poppy!" the Trolls shouted back happily. They loved their queen, and they couldn't wait for her announcement. What would it be about? A party? A holiday? A celebration? They were all good bets.

"On this beautiful morning, it gives me great pleasure to announce"—Poppy took a little pause and the Trolls leaned forward, listening intently—"A DANCE!" she exclaimed,

throwing her arms open wide in excitement.

All the Trolls cheered. They LOVED dances! With loud music, bright lights, and tasty snacks! The louder, brighter, and tastier, the better!

Even Branch cheered. Standing next to him, DJ Suki was a little surprised. He was usually so serious. She'd never seen Branch at a dance—at least, not that she could remember.

"You're excited about a dance, Branch?" she asked.

"Sure!" he answered. "Why wouldn't I be?"

"Oh, I don't know," DJ Suki said, hesitating. She didn't want to hurt Branch's feelings. "It's just that I don't think I've ever seen you dance. Do you like dancing?"

"Hey, I've got some moves," Branch said. He demonstrated, pumping his arms and

moving his feet stiffly. He bumped into a couple of Trolls in the crowd. "Oops, sorry."

"Are you okay?" one of them asked with concern in her voice. "Do you need medical attention?"

"No," Branch growled. "I'm fine. Just practicing my dance moves."

"Ohhhh," the other Troll said. "Cool!"

Up onstage, Poppy paced back and forth in anticipation. "Everyone's invited, and I thought it'd be really fun if people got together to come up with special dances! Form a group, practice a routine, and then perform it for everybody at our big dance! Doesn't that sound fun?"

The Trolls cheered again. That DID sound fun!

"All right!" Poppy said. "I'll see you in three

days at the BIG DANCE!" Music played, and Poppy danced off the stage, waving to everyone.

The Trolls gave a final cheer and immediately broke into small groups to discuss Poppy's announcement. Cooper and Guy Diamond were especially amped up. They both loved getting their grooves on!

"Hey, Guy," Cooper asked his glittery friend. "Wanna work up a fantastic dance routine with me that'll totally dazzle the crowd?"

"I was just going to ask you the same thing!" Guy said in his unmistakable shimmery voice, which sounded as though it had been electronically tuned with a soundboard. "Let's do it!"

"Great!" Cooper said. "When should we make up our new dance?"

"What's wrong with right now?" Guy asked.

"Nothing! Nothing's wrong with right now! Right now's perfect!" Cooper said. "I've already got one smooth move in mind. Check it!" He balanced on one foot, tucked his three other feet under his fuzzy stomach, and spun in a circle.

"That's great!" Guy cried. "Let's go work at my studio. It's got a disco ball!"

"Good idea!" Cooper agreed. "After you, Guy Diamond!" The two friends ran to Guy's dance studio.

Guy's studio was the perfect place to come up with a dance. It had a big open floor with plenty of room. On the walls were mirrors so they could see themselves move. A mirror ball hung from the ceiling, reflecting the lights and instantly creating a fun party mood.

"How do we start?" Cooper asked. He'd been to plenty of dances and done lots of dancing, but he'd never made up a routine before. He'd always just moved one foot and let the other three follow.

Guy offered Cooper a glass of cool water. "First we make sure we're well hydrated," he explained. "Dancing can be thirsty work!"

Cooper drained the glass and smacked his lips. "Ahhh! Thank you!"

"Now we have two choices," Guy said. "We can either pick the music and make up a dance that fits, or come up with some grooves and choose the music that matches it."

Cooper nodded, impressed. He wouldn't have thought of that in a million years. When it came to making up a dance routine, Guy Diamond clearly knew what he was doing.

"Which do you suggest?" he asked.

Guy thought for a moment. "Well," he said. "Let's try out some moves first, since we each have our own favorite steps. Then we'll pick the right music that goes with them!"

"I totally agree!" Cooper said, smiling. "And speaking of favorite moves, check THESE out!"

Cooper showed Guy all his best dance moves—twirling, jumping, kicking, and sliding—putting all four of his legs to good use. Guy applauded, then showed Cooper his moves, most of which involved flinging glitter. By the time he was done, Cooper was covered in the shiny stuff.

They loved each other's style. Each thought

the other was a terrific dancer. "This is going to be SO AWESOME!" Guy enthused.

But as they tried to learn each other's moves, they slowly realized they had a problem.

Cooper had four legs, and Guy couldn't copy many of his steps with just two legs. Plus, a lot of Cooper's best moves called for a long neck. And since Guy had a unique ability to send glitter flying everywhere, Cooper couldn't copy his signature moves.

How were they supposed to make up an impressive routine if they couldn't do each other's dances?

"Gee," Cooper said sadly. "Maybe we can't be a team, Guy. Maybe we're just too different from each other."

Guy sat on a small stool and stared up at the

slowly spinning mirror ball. He thought hard. Then he got an idea.

"If there were THREE of us, two dancers could match each other while the dancer in the middle did his special, uncopyable move! It'd look GREAT!"

"But, Guy," Cooper objected, sitting on another stool, "there AREN'T three of us! There's me—that's one—and there's you— that's another one. Together, that's two. Not three." Cooper wasn't always very confident of his math skills, so he was proud of himself for adding this up.

"I know!" Guy said. "That's why we need to add a third Troll! And we'd better hurry, before every dancer in Troll Village has already joined another team!"

"Who should we ask?"

They sat there thinking. Then Guy's face brightened.

"I know who would be PERFECT!" he shouted, jumping to his feet.

CHAPTER TWO

In the bakery, Biggie was busy whipping up a big batch of yummy cookies. His pet worm, Mr. Dinkles, watched from his perch on a nearby shelf.

"I'm experimenting with some new frosting colors," Biggie said. "Brighter than ever before!" He pointed to three bowls full of frosting. One was bright pink. Another was bright green. And the third was bright blue. They were so bright, it seemed they might glow in the dark.

"What do you think, Mr. Dinkles?" Biggie asked.

The worm stared at the bowls of frosting. The colors reflected in his big eyes.

"Mew," he said.

"Thank you!" Biggie said. "I think they're beautiful, too! I just hope everyone else likes them."

He found his favorite spatula—the one with his name on the handle—and moved the three bowls near some cooling racks that held cookies shaped like mushrooms and toadstools. (Even the youngest Troll knew the subtle difference between the two.)

"I think I'll start with . . . pink!" Biggie said happily, dipping his spatula into the bowl of bright pink frosting. "It's almost the color of Queen Poppy's hair!"

As he carefully spread the frosting on the cookies, Biggie chatted away to Mr. Dinkles. It was his habit to talk to his pet worm while he worked in the bakery. And Mr. Dinkles was an excellent listener.

"Speaking of Queen Poppy, what did you think of her announcement this morning? You know, about the big dance?"

"Mew," Mr. Dinkles said.

"Yes, it's exciting," Biggie agreed, "but to tell the truth, dances make me a little bit nervous." He finished a batch of pink cookies, rinsed off his spatula, and started spreading bright green frosting on cookies shaped like leaves.

"I mean, they're fun," Biggie continued.

"But I'm not sure I'm very good at dancing. At dances I mostly just hold you and sway back and forth. And since *you* look so good all the time, no one really notices what *I'm* doing."

"Mew!" Mr. Dinkles said.

"You're welcome," Biggie said. "Anyway, please don't tell anyone I'm nervous about my dancing. That can just be our little secret, okay?"

"Mew mew mew," Mr. Dinkles said.

"WHAT? You're going to tell everyone?" Biggie cried. "Please, Mr. Dinkles, don't do that!"

"Mew mew," Mr. Dinkles said. "Mew mew mew mew."

"Oh, you're joking! Whew!" Biggie sighed, relieved. "I get it! Good one!"

DING! DING! The doorbell rang.

"Hi, Biggie! Hi, Mr. Dinkles!" Poppy said happily when Biggie answered the door.

"Mew!" Mr. Dinkles sang out.

"Poppy!" Biggie exclaimed, giving her a big hug. "What can I do for you?"

Poppy noticed the brightly colored cookies. "Ooh!" she cooed. "These new frosting colors are BEAUTIFUL!"

"You really think so?" Biggie said, pleased.

"Oh, yeah," Poppy said. "Gorgeous!"

"Try one!" Biggie urged.

"Thank you!" Poppy picked up a bright pink cookie that matched her hair and bit into it. *CRUNCH!* She grinned. "They taste even better than they look, Biggie!"

"Thank you," he said, blushing. "I'm glad you like them."

She took another bite and spoke with her mouth full, cookie crumbs dropping onto her dress. "Anyway, you asked what you could do for me. I thought maybe you could bake some cupcakes and cookies for the big dance!"

Biggie clapped. "That's a wonderful idea! I'd be happy to!"

"Are you excited about the dance?" she asked, finishing off the cookie and licking her fingertips. "'Cause I sure am!"

Biggie and Mr. Dinkles exchanged a quick look. The big blue Troll had no intention of telling Queen Poppy that her idea was making him nervous.

"Oh, totally!" he gushed. "SO excited!" Then he added, under his breath so only Mr. Dinkles could hear, "To bake. Not to dance."

Poppy grinned. "Great! Are you going to come up with a special dance?"

"Well, I . . ."

DING! DING! The doorbell rang again. It was Guy Diamond and Cooper.

"BIGGIE!" Cooper gasped, breathing hard from running the whole way there.

"Have you joined a dance crew yet?" Guy blurted out.

"Um, no . . . ," Biggie said hesitantly. "Why do you ask?"

"Because we want you to join ours!" Cooper said. "Please?"

Biggie was shocked. Why would anyone want him to join their dance crew? He was known for his baking, not his dancing. "Why do you want me on your team?" he asked.

"Just picture it!" Guy said enthusiastically. "Me, the glitteriest Troll around! Cooper, the coolest multilegged Troll ever! And YOU—the tallest, bluest Troll in the village! We'll look fantastic dancing together! No one will be able to take their eyes off us!"

"Exactly!" Cooper agreed. "What do you say? Will you join us?"

"W-w-well," Biggie stammered. "I don't know. . . ."

Poppy touched Biggie's arm. "Biggie, this is terrific!"

"Yeah," Biggie murmured, still unsure. "Terrific . . ."

"So is that a yes?" Guy asked.

He and Cooper leaned toward Biggie, holding their breath. So did Poppy. Even Mr.

Dinkles wiggled closer to hear Biggie's answer.

"Sure," Biggie sighed. "That's a yes."

"YAY!" Cooper, Guy, and Poppy cheered, patting him on the back and shaking his hands.

"Mew," Mr. Dinkles said.

CHAPTER THREE

"Gotta go!" Poppy said, waving over her shoulder as she headed for the door. "Bridget's coming for her weekly visit. Have fun with your dance routine. I just know it's going to be utterly amazing!"

Biggie waved goodbye as he watched her leave. He was a little stunned at how quickly things were moving. He could hardly believe he was going to be on a team with Cooper and Guy

Diamond—two of the village's best dancers!

"Come on, Biggie!" Cooper said enthusiastically. "Let's go to Guy's studio and start working!" He took Biggie by the hand and tried to pull him toward the door, but Biggie wouldn't budge.

"I have to finish frosting these cookies," Biggie said.

"We can help you!" Guy offered. Before Biggie could argue, Guy and Cooper had grabbed a couple of spatulas and were spreading the bright blue frosting on cookies shaped like flowers. With all three of them working together, the cookies were frosted in no time.

"There!" Cooper said, licking his spatula, "All done! Let's go! Zip-zippity-zip!"

But Biggie still hesitated. "Queen Poppy

asked me to make cupcakes and cookies for the big dance. I should probably start working on those. . . ."

Guy Diamond shook his head firmly. "There's PLENTY of time to make those later! Besides, you want them to be fresh, not stale and dried-out!"

"Dance now, bake later!" Cooper chimed in. "Right, Mr. Dinkles?"

"Mew!" Mr. Dinkles agreed.

Biggie shot his beloved pet worm a look that said *"How COULD you?"* He sighed. "Okay. You two go ahead. I'll be right there."

"Time to get our dance on!" Guy said, grooving out of the cupcakery. Cooper was right behind him.

Biggie turned to Mr. Dinkles. "Okay, my

friend. Do you want to come along or stay here?"

"Mew," Mr. Dinkles said.

"That's fine," Biggie said, "but if you get lonely, just pay Poppy a visit. She's always glad to see you!"

"Mew mew mew," Mr. Dinkles said.

"I am NOT stalling!" Biggie protested. He gave his pet worm a hug and headed out the door.

As the three friends hustled through the village toward Guy's studio, Biggie thought of something that might delay the practice. "What music are we going to dance to?" he asked.

"We haven't decided yet," Cooper said. "Guy says you can either start with the music or the moves. We tried starting with our best moves."

"Did that work?" Biggie asked.

Cooper frowned. "Not exactly. Our best moves are really different from each other's."

"Then maybe we should try starting with the music," Biggie suggested, "and set our routine to the song. I was thinking we could ask DJ Suki for something good."

Guy smiled big, and glitter on his teeth sparkled in the sunshine. "That's a great idea, Biggie! DJ Suki's the best! I KNEW you were going to be a great addition to our dance crew!"

So Guy, Cooper, and Biggie turned around and headed off to DJ Suki's pod, where she had put together all her best beats and tracks. As they got closer to her place, they could hear thudding bass notes. *BOOM! BUH-BOOM PAH-BOOM! BOOM! BUH-BOOM PAH-BOOM!*

Fuzzbert was leaving as they approached the

front door. He called back to DJ Suki, thanking her in his own special language of grunts and growls. "GRUNK ERNK HUNH DERN MERZERK!" Then he danced down the path, hopping and spinning, nodding the tip of his hair to Cooper, Guy, and Biggie as he passed them.

"Looks like we're not the only ones who had the idea of coming to DJ Suki for some music," Cooper noted.

"Fuzzbert's an amazing dancer!" Guy said. "Nobody moves like he does!"

"Or talks like him," Biggie added.

"Or LOOKS like him!" Cooper said. "Fuzzbert's the fuzziest!"

They went inside. Wearing her earphones, DJ Suki was working the turntables on her

Wooferbug, nodding in time to the pounding beats. She couldn't hear anything but the music, and she was concentrating so hard that she didn't notice her three friends come in.

"DJ—" Biggie said, touching her arm.

"WHOA!" she yelled. *ZZZZRITTT!* Her Wooferbug scratched to a halt.

"I'm sorry!" Biggie cried. "I didn't mean to startle you. Did you scratch your Wooferbug? Is he okay?"

DJ Suki took off her earphones and patted her Wooferbug's fuzzy side. "Oh, he's fine! He LIKES scratches! See?"

She scratched under the Wooferbug's chin, and he responded with happy little sighs and whistles.

"So," DJ Suki said, "I'm guessing you're

here for a kickin' new piece of music to go with your special routine for the big dance!"

Cooper's eyes widened. "How did you know that? Are you a mind reader? Ooh! What am I thinking about right now?" He leaned over to her and whispered, "I'll give you a hint: it's cupcakes!"

DJ Suki laughed. "No, I'm not a mind reader! It's just that EVERYONE has been coming to me all morning asking for tunes to dance to!"

"Oh, no," Biggie said, trying not to sound relieved. "Are you all out?"

She laughed again. "Of course not! I NEVER run out of music! There are always more beats, more tunes, and more ways to put them together! Music goes on and on! What kind of song did you have in mind?"

Guy Diamond stepped forward. "We were thinking something with a great beat and a hook that you can dance to—a piece that will get stuck in people's minds and drive them crazy!"

DJ nodded. "That's just the kind of music I like, too! Let's see . . . maybe something like this?"

She made some quick adjustments to several of the musical critters in her pod, then moved her hands over the turntables on the back of her Wooferbug. A fast beat started thumping. Then a tune played over the beat.

Cooper and Guy bobbed their heads in time to the music. They moved around the pod, trying out different steps.

"I love it!" Cooper said.

"Me too!" Guy agreed, leaving a trail of

glitter across the floor as he danced.

Biggie wasn't sure. The music seemed awfully fast to him.

"But is it fast enough?" Guy asked.

Biggie started to say he thought the music was TOO fast, but DJ Suki spoke up before Biggie.

"Oh, I can make it faster!" DJ Suki assured Guy. She made a quick adjustment, and the music sped up to a furious pace.

"Yeah!" Cooper said, running around in time to the music.

"That's what I'm talking about!" Guy cheered, moving his feet so fast, they were a glittery blur.

Biggie gulped.

When the tune ended, Guy, Cooper, and

even Biggie applauded. DJ Suki took a little bow. She handed them a fuzzy little Tunebug who'd memorized the tune to take with them.

"When you three dance to this," she said, "the crowd will go wild!"

They thanked her over and over, then headed for Guy's studio to work on their routine.

Biggie still wasn't ready. As they trotted along, he thought of something else they could do before they started practicing.

"What are we going to wear to the big dance?" he asked.

The others paused. They hadn't really thought about it.

"Hats?" Cooper suggested.

"Nothing but my smile," Guy offered.

"That's great," Biggie said. "But I was

thinking maybe we should wear special matching outfits. I'm sure Satin and Chenille would love to make something really nice for us."

Cooper clapped Biggie on the back. "Great thinking, Biggie! You are on fire today in the brains department!"

"I agree!" Guy said, nodding. "As soon as we've worked up our dance routine, we'll go ask Satin and Chenille about making us some stylish new outfits."

Guy continued walking toward his studio, but Biggie stood still.

"Remember how a bunch of people had already gone to DJ Suki for music when we got there?" he asked. "Maybe if we don't go to Satin and Chenille right away, they'll already be too busy making outfits for other dancers."

"Hmm," Cooper mused. "That is a definite possibility."

"And besides," Biggie went on, "even if they're not too busy, Satin and Chenille will need time to make our outfits, so the sooner we ask them, the better. At least in my opinion."

Guy nodded. "You've convinced me, Biggie. To the Fashion Twins' Super Threads pod!"

CHAPTER FOUR

When Guy, Biggie, and Cooper reached the twins' pod, they were happy to see no Trolls there ahead of them. As usual, Satin and Chenille were working on new outfits, measuring fabric and sewing on buttons. When they saw their friends, they dropped what they were doing and ran to the door.

"Come in!" Satin said.

"Come in!" Chenille echoed.

The twins stood in the doorway, pink Satin on the left and blue Chenille on the right, their connected hair arched above them. Guy and Cooper easily walked under the arch, while Biggie had to duck. He'd always thought it might be fun to play jump rope with the twins swinging their hair around, but he hadn't had the nerve to ask them. Besides, what if he tripped?

"What can we . . . ," Satin began.

". . . help you with?" Chenille finished.

Guy explained that the three of them planned to perform a dance routine, so they thought it might be a good idea to wear . . .

"Matching outfits!" Satin interrupted, excited at the thought.

"Designed and made by us, the fashion twins!" Chenille said, equally excited.

The girls whipped out their tape measures. As they measured their friends, they rapidly tossed ideas back and forth to each other.

"I'm thinking . . . ," Satin began.

". . . vests? And pants?" Chenille finished.

"Yes!" Satin agreed. "But short pants or long pants?"

Once they'd come up with a basic design, they started choosing materials, digging through piles of fabrics and draping them across every piece of furniture in the room. When they ran out of furniture, they tossed the pieces of cloth over the dancers' heads and shoulders. Then they walked around the guys, rubbing the fabrics between their fingers, trying to decide what would look best.

"It has to be . . . ," Chenille began.

". . . dazzling!" Satin finished. "Stunning! Magical! Luminous!"

"Agreed!" Chenille said.

Biggie started to worry about the outfits the twins were describing. All he ever wore was a purple vest and purple shorts. That was his look. Now Satin and Chenille were talking about long pants, jackets, capes, hoods, and scarves in materials that shimmered and glittered, with ruffles and feathers! What would Biggie look like in a getup like that? How would he feel? Had it been a mistake to ask the twins for help? Secretly, he'd only suggested it to put off learning the dance a little longer. He hadn't thought about what the twins would design.

Cooper seemed to love everything they came up with. He had only one request: "Can I wear my hat?"

The twins squinted at his hat, trying to decide

whether it would work with their ensemble ideas.

"What if we made one just like it," Satin said slowly, "only . . ."

". . . flashier?" Chenille said.

"Like with sequins?" Satin said.

"And feathers?" Chenille suggested.

"That sounds so AWESOME!" Cooper exclaimed.

Guy Diamond was also enthusiastic about the twins' ideas—even though he preferred being naked. "Will my costume have lots of glitter?" he asked.

Satin and Chenille laughed. "I'm pretty sure whatever you wear ALWAYS ends up covered in glitter!" Satin said.

Finally, the twins were satisfied with their

designs. "We'll have your outfits ready . . . ," Satin began.

". . . on the day of the big dance!" Chenille finished.

The dance team thanked the twins and left.

"Okay," Guy said when they were outside. "Let's hit the dance floor!"

Biggie couldn't think of any more distracting errands. He couldn't put the dancing off any longer. It was now or never. . . .

At Guy's studio, the three Trolls got to work on their routine.

"It can really be anything," Cooper said, "as long as it's the greatest dance the world has ever seen!"

They tapped the fuzzy little music bug DJ

Suki had sent with them, and the fast song she'd created blared out into the studio. Matching the rapid beat of the music, Cooper and Guy did their signature moves—kicks, splits, spins, jumps, and handstands.

Biggie did his own signature move, planting his feet on the ground and swaying from side to side, trying to keep up with the quick tempo.

"Great!" Guy cheered. "Those are the solo moves we can each do when we're in the middle! Now we just have to come up with a dance we'll all be doing when we're NOT in the middle. I was thinking maybe something like this. . . ."

Guy started to do a complicated dance with lots of spins, slides, and cross-steps. Remembering that the other two couldn't shake off glitter the way he could, he left his typical glitter-producing steps out.

Fascinated, Cooper grinned and watched carefully, bobbing his head to the music. He moved his feet, trying to copy Guy's steps. His front and back feet made the same motions, smoothly turning Guy's two-footed moves into four-footed moves. When it came to picking up dance steps, Cooper was quick. Before too long, he was mimicking Guy perfectly.

Biggie wasn't.

He just stared at Guy with his mouth open. How could he ever learn all those complicated movements? By the time he'd sort of understood the first step, Guy had already progressed to the next, and the next, and the next. So many steps! So many moves! How could just one little dance have so many parts to it? When DJ Suki had played her song for them at her studio, it had seemed kind of short. But now that Biggie faced the task of learning all these steps, the song seemed to go on forever!

"What do you think?" Guy asked when he was done, breathing just a tiny bit harder than someone who'd been on a leisurely stroll.

"Fabulous!" Cooper shouted.

"Very . . . complex," Biggie said in a small voice.

"Now all we have to do is remember what I just did!" Guy said, laughing. "Come on—let's all do it together!"

Guy started the music again. He began doing his dance, and Cooper joined in, looking down at Guy's feet, matching what he was doing.

Biggie *tried* to match Guy, but he just couldn't keep up.

Guy realized they were going too fast for Biggie.

"That's okay," he said reassuringly. "No problem! Let's try it without the music, and we'll go through the steps one by one, slowly."

"Thank you!" Biggie said, smiling. This sounded more like it!

But it was still hard.

Guy counted out the beats. "One, two, three, four. One, two, three, four . . ." As he said each number, he did another step. Sometimes instead of saying the number, he'd describe the step. "One, two, three, kick! One, two, three, spin!"

Biggie still couldn't get it. It seemed that he was always kicking when he was supposed to be spinning, and spinning when he was supposed to be kicking. He kept tripping over his own feet.

He also realized that Guy and Cooper were much better at *doing* dances than *describing* them. Whenever he asked them how to do part of the dance, instead of explaining it, they'd just say, "Like this!" And then they'd do the step perfectly.

But they really were trying to help Biggie learn the dance. They tried all the teaching methods they could think of. They broke the dance down into little bits. They stood right in front of Biggie and demonstrated the steps as slowly as possible. They tried teaching him the end of the dance, and then the part just before the end, and then the part just before that, so he'd be heading toward the section of the dance he already knew, instead of journeying into the scary unknown with every step. They grabbed his feet and moved them for him. They even tried drawing glitter footprints on the floor for him to follow.

Nothing worked.

After what seemed like the thousandth time through the routine, Biggie's face felt hot. His jaw was tight. He had a lump in his throat. *Why can't I learn this dance as easily as Guy and Cooper?* he thought. All of a sudden, he felt tears spring to his eyes.

"I'm sorry!" he sobbed. "I've gotta go!"

Biggie ran out of Guy's studio, crying.

"Wait, Biggie!" Cooper called after him.

"Come back!" Guy cried.

But he was gone.

CHAPTER FIVE

Biggie thought about running to the bakery, but he didn't want to upset Mr. Dinkles with his tears. Besides, if Guy and Cooper came looking for him, that would be the first place they'd check.

Instead, he ran through the village (luckily, he didn't bump into anyone) and into the forest. He kept going until he came to a little clearing. He plopped onto a stump and sobbed, covering his face with his hands.

"What's the matter?" said a kind voice.

Biggie looked up, wiping away his tears. He saw King Peppy standing there, leaning on a cane, smiling at him.

"I was out for a little walk in the woods, and I heard you crying. Anything I can help with?" the old Troll asked gently.

"Not unless you're the world's greatest dance teacher," Biggie said miserably.

King Peppy looked surprised. "Huh!" he said. "That's not what I expected you to say! Well, when it comes to dancing, I guess I used to be all right, a long time ago."

He did a little shuffling step, kicking up a few leaves and acorns. Then he winced.

"Ouch!" He reached around to massage his lower back with his fingers. "I guess I'm a little too old for the dances I used to do."

King Peppy sat on a toadstool near Biggie. "Even back in the days when I was a pretty good dancer, I don't remember ever trying to *teach* anyone how to dance. Is that what's got you upset? Do you need to know how to teach dancing?"

Biggie shook his head slowly. "No, King Peppy. I don't need to know how to teach dancing. I need to know how to *learn* dancing."

"Oh." King Peppy nodded. "I see." Then he shook his head. "No, I don't. I don't see. Maybe you'd better explain from the beginning."

Biggie hadn't thought he wanted to talk about his problem. But there was something about King Peppy's gentle voice and his kind eyes that made Biggie feel he could tell the old Troll just about anything and he wouldn't think it was silly, no matter what. So Biggie explained about Queen Poppy's big dance.

"Yes, I know about that," said King Peppy. "My daughter told me all about it at breakfast. She is very excited!"

Biggie went on to tell the king about Guy and Cooper's invitation to join their dance crew, and DJ Suki's song, and Satin and Chenille's outfits, and how Biggie just couldn't learn his team members' dance, no matter how hard he tried.

"I guess I'm just no good at dancing," Biggie said, about to cry again. When he said "dancing," his voice cracked.

"Oh, I doubt that very much!" King Peppy said, handing Biggie a light-blue handkerchief.

Biggie blew his nose. *HOOONNK!* He

offered the soggy handkerchief back to King Peppy.

"Keep it," the old Troll said. "I think you're a clever Troll who can do anything he puts his mind to. I've been in your bakery. I've eaten your cupcakes, and your cookies, and your pies. Why, when it comes to baking, you're a genius!"

"Thank you," Biggie said, smiling a shy smile and blushing a little.

"I've also seen all those pictures you've taken of your pet worm. What's his name?"

"Mr. Dinkles."

"Right! Mr. Dinkles! You're smart when it comes to photography, too! And all those little costumes you make for him—it takes a clever brain to think of things like that, Biggie."

Part of being a good leader is being able to recognize what people are good at and bring out the best in them. King Peppy had been a good leader for a long time, so he knew he could make Biggie feel better about himself just by telling him the truth.

"Thanks, King Peppy," Biggie said, smiling. Then he frowned. "But I *still* can't learn that dance, even if I can bake and take pictures and make costumes for Mr. Dinkles. Maybe I'm just not clever when it comes to dancing. Oh, dear. . . ." The bighearted Troll felt more tears in his eyes. He wiped his cheeks and blew his nose again. *HONK!*

King Peppy was quiet for a moment. Something was coming back to him. Something he hadn't thought about in many years . . .

"You know," he said to Biggie, "a long, long time ago, I heard about a song."

"A song?" Biggie asked, puzzled. He didn't see what an old song had to do with his dancing problem.

"Yes, but not just any song. A song that gets stuck in your head and drives you crazy," the king said. "A *magical* song."

"Magical?" Biggie was intrigued. "How magical? You mean like it would cast a spell on you?"

"Well, kind of," King Peppy said. "But not exactly. Once you learned this song and sang it all the way through, you could master any dance, no matter how complicated and difficult it was."

"Really?" Biggie said, sitting up straight.

"That sounds wonderful! Will you teach it to me? Please?"

"No," King Peppy said. "I'm afraid not."

"Why not?" Biggie asked, slumping. "Oh, I get it. You think I should learn the dance on my own. That it'll be a good challenge for me, and that I shouldn't just master the dance with a magical song."

King Peppy looked surprised. "What? No, that's not it at all! I won't teach you the song because I can't! I don't remember it!"

"Oh," Biggie said. "Well, do you know anyone who *does* remember this magical song?"

King Peppy squinted, thinking hard. Then he opened his eyes wide.

"Yes!" he cried. "I do!"

CHAPTER SIX

Biggie leaned forward eagerly. "Who?

"Herman."

"Herman? Who's Herman?"

"Herman the hermit," King Peppy explained. "The old Troll who lives all by himself on the far edge of the village."

Biggie looked doubtful. "The one who never, ever talks to anyone? Who runs and hides in his hole under a tree anytime someone tries to ask him anything?"

"That's the one!" King Peppy said brightly.

Nearby, they heard two voices calling, "Biggie! Biggie, where are you?" It was Cooper and Guy.

"Sounds like they're looking for you," King Peppy said.

"Yes," Biggie sighed. "They're on my dance crew."

"They sound worried," the king said.

Biggie looked concerned. "I didn't mean to worry them. Guy! Cooper!" he called. "I'm over here!"

Moments later, Cooper and Guy rushed into the clearing.

"Biggie!" Cooper said. "Thank goodness you're all right!" He noticed King Peppy. "Oh, hi, King Peppy! Nice to see you!"

Guy put a hand on Biggie's shoulder.

"Biggie, we're sorry we pushed you too fast to learn the dance. We never meant to make you feel bad. Dancing should always be fun!"

"No, I'm sorry," Biggie insisted. "I should have told you how nervous I was about learning the dance. But now everything's going to be all right!"

He told them about the magical song that helped you easily learn any dance. He only had to get the old hermit Troll to teach it to him.

"Amazing!" Guy exclaimed. "I've never heard of such a song!"

"That sounds great!" Cooper cheered. "Come on! Let's go ask the hermit right now!" He was ready to run back through the forest and across the village to the hermit's tree. But Biggie stopped him.

"It's not that simple," Biggie explained. "You can't just burst in on a hermit. He'll hide deep in the roots under his tree and refuse to come out."

"That makes sense," Guy said. "So what's the best way to talk to a hermit?"

"I don't know," Biggie admitted. "What do you think, King Peppy?"

The old Troll stroked his pink-and-white beard. "Well," he said, "I haven't talked to the old guy in years. But I think I know someone who has. He might be able to give you some good advice about how to approach Herman without scaring him off. . . ."

~~~~~~

In his underground bunker, Branch brought mugs of bloomingflower tea to his friends.

"Yes," he said. "King Peppy's right. I did talk to the hermit. It was back before we became friends with the Bergens. I'd heard that he knew a thing or two about Bergens, so I went to see if he'd share his knowledge with me. I figured the more I knew about Bergens, the safer I'd be when they showed up again."

Biggie sipped his tea. *SLURRP!* "So Herman was willing to talk to you?"

Branch shook his head and chuckled. "Not at first. In fact, not for a long time."

Cooper, Guy, and Biggie exchanged worried looks. They didn't *have* a long time. The big dance was coming up soon.

"But eventually," Branch continued, "I discovered a way to make him feel comfortable about coming out of his cave."

"And what was that?" Biggie asked eagerly.

"Hugs?" Cooper guessed.

Branch shook his head, disgusted. "No, not hugs! He's not fond of hugs! Do NOT hug the hermit!"

"Even at Hug Time?" Cooper asked, amazed.

"ESPECIALLY at Hug Time!" Branch warned.

"Weird!" Cooper said.

"So tell us, Branch," Guy said, trying to get the conversation back on track. "How did you get the old hermit to talk to you?"

Branch smiled. "I brought him a gift. His favorite thing—something he couldn't resist."

"Hugs?" Cooper guessed again.

"NO! NOT HUGS!" Branch barked. "I TOLD YOU, HE DOES *NOT* LIKE HUGS!"

Cooper shrugged. "*I* like hugs."

Biggie set his empty mug down. "What's the hermit's favorite thing?"

"Sweetbug Sticky Sap," he said. "He can't get enough of it. Bring the hermit a jar full of Sweetbug Sticky Sap and he'll tell you just about anything you want to know."

"I don't blame him!" Cooper said, smiling. "Sweetbug Sticky Sap is the best!"

Guy and Biggie nodded. All Trolls loved Sweetbug Sticky Sap—when they could get it. Sweetbugs were shy, so their homes were hard to find. And they liked to bite.

"You wouldn't happen to have a spare jar of Sweetbug Sticky Sap, would you?" Biggie asked hopefully.

Branch shook his head. "Nope. Don't you

have some at the bakery?" he asked.

"No," Biggie said. "It's hard to come by."

"True," Branch agreed. "Well, I can tell you where the Sweetbugs were when I went to gather the sap for the hermit. But be careful. Those Sweetbug bites really hurt!"

ꬹꬹꬹꬹꬹꬹꬹ

Following Branch's directions, Biggie, Guy, and Cooper hurried to the flowery meadow where he'd found the Sweetbugs. Once they got there, they heard a low-pitched drone.

"Sweetbugs!" Biggie whispered. "Branch said they make a droning sound!"

"Right before they bite you?" Cooper asked nervously.

The three Trolls cautiously made their way to the far corner of the meadow, where the droning seemed to be the loudest. In a thick clump of flowers, they spotted the Sweetbugs' home— a cluster of boxes made of a waxy substance.

"Branch said they keep the Sweetbug Sticky Sap in the round chamber," Guy whispered. "All we have to do is go in and fill our jar."

The Trolls had to tiptoe all the way around the waxy chamber before they found a small opening. Biggie could barely squeeze through, but he made it. Vats full of sweet, sticky sap lined the walls. They quickly filled their jar and slipped back out.

"Made it!" Cooper said, breathing a big sigh of relief. "And we didn't see even one Sweetbug!"

Suddenly, the droning got much louder. . . .

"Look!" Biggie said, pointing toward the

boxes behind them. Sweetbugs were flying out of their houses and zooming right at the Trolls in an angry swarm! Each Sweetbug was bigger than Biggie, with a mouth full of gleaming, snapping teeth! *CHOMP! CHOMP! CHOMP!*

"RUN!" Guy screamed. As the Trolls dashed away, Guy blew a cloud of glitter back toward the Sweetbugs. The glitter filled the bugs' snapping mouths and covered their bodies.

When the Sweetbugs stopped chasing the Trolls to concentrate on cleaning off the glitter, Cooper, Biggie, and Guy ran all the way back to the village. Finally, they stopped to catch their breath, huffing and puffing as they leaned over and put their hands on their knees.

Biggie held up the jar of Sweetbug Sticky Sap. "We got it!"

"And not one bite!" Cooper said. "I didn't tell you guys before, but I really don't like getting bitten."

"Neither do we," Biggie said.

"Really?" Cooper said, surprised. "No wonder we make such a great team!"

"Okay!" Guy said. "Now we have to find that hermit."

CHAPTER SEVEN

A couple of days later, the friends set out to track down the hermit. They all knew where he lived: deep in the roots under an enormous old tree at the far edge of Troll Village. It was easy enough to find the tall, gnarled tree, but picking their way through its twisted roots was like finding their way through a maze. Luckily, Branch had described the path to Herman's dwelling in great detail.

As they stepped along a bumpy, curving root,

they spotted a jumble of rocks ahead. Between two of the rocks they saw a narrow opening, just as Branch had described. The opening led to the hermit's cave beneath the old tree.

"There it is!" Biggie said, pointing.

"Come on, let's run!" Cooper said excitedly.

They sprinted across the rest of the root and toward the opening in the rocks. But just before they reached it—*WHOOSH!* All three were hoisted into the air, trapped in a net made of sturdy green vines.

"Whoa!" they yelled. "What's happening? Help! Let us out of here!"

They dangled there for a moment, swaying in front of the jumble of rocks. Then a raspy voiced creaked, "Now, what do we have here?"

An old Troll with a long gray beard emerged

from the opening. He was short—not much taller than Smidge. He walked slowly, with a rolling, side-to-side motion, as though he were trying to keep his balance on a ship sailing over rough seas. He circled the net hanging in the air, studying the Trolls caught inside.

"Mm-hmm," he mumbled to himself. "Mm-hmm." When he'd walked all the way around the net, he straightened up a little, as if he'd come to a conclusion. "Trolls. Three of 'em."

"Yes, sir," Guy said politely. "We are Trolls, just as you are, and we've come to pay you a friendly visit."

"Don't like visitors," Herman growled. "Why do you think I live way out here under a tree?"

"We just wanted to ask you one little

question," Cooper blurted out. "If you'd kindly lower this net and set us free—"

"Don't like questions," the hermit grumbled. "Seems like anytime someone asks me a question, they expect me to answer it!"

Finally, Biggie managed to free his arm and hold up the jar of Sweetbug Sticky Sap. "We brought you a present!" he said. "Sweetbug Sticky Sap!"

Herman's eyes got big and the corners of his mouth raised a tiny bit. His arms shot forward and he wiggled his fingers. "THANK YOU!"

Biggie hugged the jar to his chest. "You're welcome! And we'll be happy to give you this present . . . just as soon as you let us out of your trap!"

A squeaky sound that might have been

laughter came out of the old Troll. He stepped behind a rock and loosened a vine. *WHOMP!* The net fell to the ground with the three Trolls in it. They stood up and untangled themselves from the vines.

"Come in! Come in!" Herman cried, waving for them to follow him through the narrow opening between the rocks. "Bring that jar of Sweetbug Sticky Sap with you. But don't drop it! That stuff's mighty hard to come by. Especially if you never leave your home! Which I strongly recommend, by the way."

The guys brushed themselves off and followed the old hermit into his cave. It was a tight squeeze through the entrance, especially for Biggie, but they made it.

Inside, the light was dim, but they could see

a small space filled with bits of moss, twigs, pebbles, and leaves. In its own way, it was cozy.

"Sit down! Sit down!" Herman insisted. "Anywhere you like!" There weren't seats, exactly, but the three visitors managed to perch on rocks and roots that stuck into the cave.

Biggie handed Herman the jar of Sweetbug Sticky Sap. The hermit looked grateful and licked his lips. Seeing his chance, Biggie said, "So I was talking to King Peppy, and he told me that you might know a certain song that—"

"Just a moment!" Herman said, holding up a wrinkly hand to stop him. "Before you say another word, there's something I've got to do."

"And what's that?" Biggie asked nervously.

"Make some toast!" the hermit said happily. He pulled out a small loaf of seed bread, cut off four slices, and stuck them on the ends of a branch. Then he held the bread over a tiny fire until it was golden brown. It smelled delicious.

Herman put the pieces of toast on chipped plates, carefully spread Sweetbug Sticky Sap on each piece (slathering a little extra on his own slice), and handed the plates to the Trolls.

"Thank you!" Biggie said politely. "King Peppy said that this magical song—"

"Hold your Glowflies!" Herman barked. "Can't have toast without tea!"

He brewed some butterflower tea, dripping just a few drops of Sweetbug Sticky Sap into each cup. Then he handed the cups around and raised his in the air. "To visitors!" he said. "May they come almost never, but bring Sweetbug Sticky Sap when they do!"

All four Trolls bit into the sweet toast, and it tasted just as delicious as it smelled. They sipped the tea, and that was good, too.

"Now, young man," Herman said to Biggie, settling back against a mossy rock, "what was it you wanted to ask me? I guess you've earned an answer to your question."

Biggie told Herman what King Peppy had said about the magical song that helped the singer learn any dance in the world. He was so eager to hear the song that the words tumbled out of his mouth rapidly, with hardly a single breath between them.

The old hermit sat there chewing his toast, thinking. He took a long, loud slurp of tea—*SHLUUUUURRRP!*—and set his cup down.

"Yes," he said slowly. "I know the tune you're

talking about. 'The Dancemaster's Song.' Very old. And very effective—works every time, like a charm."

Biggie was thrilled! "Will you teach it to me?" he asked eagerly.

"Nope," the old hermit said firmly.

Biggie was stunned. He'd fetched the Sticky Sap from the Sweetbugs. He'd made his way through the maze of tree roots. He'd given a jar of the Sticky Sap to Herman. He'd even waited while the hermit made toast and tea!

"Why?" he asked, deeply disappointed. "Why won't you teach me 'The Dancemaster's Song'?"

"I've forgotten it," Herman admitted.

CHAPTER EIGHT

Biggie, Cooper, and Guy sat there for a little while, taking in the bad news. They didn't feel like eating any more toast, and their tea got cold.

"Are you sure?" Guy said. "Maybe if you think about it, the song'll come back to you."

"Yeah!" Cooper said encouragingly. "Like this one time, I couldn't remember where I'd put my hat, and then I looked in the mirror and remembered I was wearing it!"

The hermit just shook his head. "I'm thinking about it, but nothing's coming back—no words, no tune, no nothing. All I can remember is that I used to know it, but now it's gone." He glanced at his empty plate. "Like my toast." He looked up brightly. "Anyone want seconds?"

Biggie sighed and stood up. "No, thank you. I guess we might as well head home. Mr. Dinkles will be waiting for me."

The three friends squeezed back through the gap between the rocks and started to cross over the bumpy root. Then they heard Herman calling after them.

"Wait! Wait!" he cried. "I've just thought of something!" He came out of his cave, waving them back.

Biggie hurried over to him. "The words to

the magical song?" he asked eagerly.

"No, not that," the hermit said, shaking his head. "But I'll tell you what: there might be a way to *make* me remember!"

"Not another jar of Sweetbug Sticky Sap, I hope," Cooper groaned. "We were lucky enough to get one without being bitten. I don't know if we can do it again. This time they'll be waiting for us!"

Herman laughed his creaky laugh. "Heh, heh, heh! No! Though if you ever *want* to bring me another jar, that'd be just fine!" He sat on a small knob sticking out of a thick root. "I mean I *might* be able to remember 'The Dancemaster's Song' if I was really and truly frightened!"

"Frightened?" Guy repeated. "Are you saying we could *scare* the song out of you?"

The hermit nodded rapidly. "That's right! That's right! Sometimes when I'm scared, old memories—like tunes and words to songs—come back to me! Brains are funny things. Especially mine! Heh, heh, heh!"

"Oh, well, that's very interesting," Cooper said slowly as he snuck around behind the old Troll. "Because my grandma used to always tell me her favorite dessert was— BOO!" He shouted the last word as loudly as he could.

Herman didn't even jump.

"Your grandmother's favorite dessert was boo?" he said, puzzled. "What's boo? And what's dessert got to do with anything, anyway?"

"I was trying to scare you," Cooper said. "You know, by— *BOO!*" This time he screamed even louder, but it didn't startle Herman a bit.

"Stop that," the hermit said calmly. "It's annoying. And bad for your throat."

"You're right," Cooper rasped. "And when I get a sore throat, it's a BIG sore throat!"

Guy motioned for Cooper and Biggie to join him. "Guys, over here. Excuse us a second, Herman."

"Certainly," Herman said politely. He sat there licking sap off his fingers.

Cooper and Biggie huddled up with Guy. "Okay," Guy whispered, "we've got to scare him, right?"

"Right," Biggie agreed.

"Yeah, but how?" Cooper asked. "I gave him my best 'boo' and he didn't even blink. He doesn't scare easily."

Guy nodded. "I know, but he had just told

us to scare him, so he was probably expecting it. He saw it coming. When you 'boo' someone, the element of surprise is very important."

Now it was Biggie and Cooper's turn to nod. What Guy was saying made sense.

"So what do we do?" Biggie asked. "We can't wait around until he's forgotten he asked us to scare him. That might take forever."

Guy glanced over at the hermit. He was still licking his fingers. "Instead of screaming 'boo' at Herman, we've got to try another way of frightening him, like dressing up as some kind of scary monster."

Cooper looked confused. "How are we supposed to do that? I didn't bring any scary monster costumes with me. Also, I don't *have* any scary monster costumes," he said.

"We'll have to put one together somehow," Guy said. "Maybe we can find something in Herman's cave." He glanced over at the old Troll again and saw that he'd nodded off. "Look! He's fallen asleep! This is our chance. Come on! But don't wake him up!"

The three Trolls broke out of their huddle and silently snuck past the dozing hermit. They squeezed through the narrow entrance and into his cave. Once inside, they looked around for inspiration.

There wasn't much.

About the only things in the hermit's cave were little bits and pieces of nature that had caught his eye on his solitary strolls through the woods: Part of a snail shell. A pebble. A piece of bark. A red leaf. A few colorful feathers.

Nothing that added up to a monster costume.

Guy noticed the ring of stones in the corner where Herman had built the small fire to toast the bread. The fire had gone cold, but there were partly burnt sticks in the stone ring. "I've got an idea!" he said.

He carefully fished a scorched stick out of the ring and blew on it to make sure it was cool. He went over to Biggie, holding the stick like a paintbrush. "Turn around," he instructed Biggie. The big Troll turned, and Guy used the soot on the end of the stick to draw a fierce face on the back of Biggie's head. It had big eyes, a pointed nose, and a mouth full of long, sharp fangs.

Then Guy used the sooty stick to draw scales across the back of Biggie's vest. "Okay," he said. "Now raise your arms and growl!"

"Growl?" Biggie asked.

"Yes, growl!" Guy repeated. "Like a ferocious monster!"

Growling didn't come naturally to Biggie, who was a gentle, sweet Troll. His first attempt at a growl sounded more like a purr.

"Make your voice deeper," Guy said.

"Yeah, like Smidge's," Cooper suggested.

"Right," Guy agreed. "And louder. Like this: GRRRRR!"

"GRRRRR!" Biggie growled in a deeper, louder voice.

"Not bad!" Guy said.

"Pretty scary!" Cooper agreed.

"Of course, you'll have to walk backward," Guy pointed out. "Think you can do that?"

Biggie wasn't sure. He hadn't spent a lot of

time walking backward. He liked to see where he was going. He took a couple of cautious steps back but tripped over a tree root and fell. *"Oof!"*

Cooper and Guy ran over and helped him up.

"Don't worry," Guy said. "We can guide you until you're right behind Herman. Then we'll wake him up, and you go into your monster act!"

"Okay," Biggie sighed. "I'll try."

The friends quietly crept out of the cave. Herman was still asleep. Biggie turned around so his back was to the hermit. Then Cooper and Guy silently guided him step by step until he was standing right behind him. Guy motioned for Biggie to raise his arms menacingly. He did, leaning backward over Herman.

As Guy shook Herman awake, he signaled

for Biggie to growl as loudly as possible.

Biggie took a deep breath and opened his mouth. *"GRRRRRRR!"*

Herman's eyes popped open. He looked up at the beast hovering over him with his arms raised. Then he peered at the face Guy had drawn on the back of Biggie's head. "What is that?" he asked. "Soot? Not bad! But also not scary!"

Biggie lowered his arms and turned around to face Herman. "You didn't happen to have any nightmares while you were napping, did you? The kind that might scare you into remembering 'The Dancemaster's Song'?" As he spoke, he rubbed the soot off the back of his head and vest.

"'Fraid not," Herman said, standing and stretching. "As a matter of fact, I had a very nice dream about eating another piece of toast with Sweetbug Sticky Sap on it. Which is an excellent idea!" He started toward the entrance to his cave.

"Wait a minute!" Biggie called. "I don't know why we didn't just ask you in the first place, Herman. What are you afraid of?"

Herman stopped in his tracks.

"Tarantapuffs?" Guy suggested. "Bluebugs?"

"Public speaking?" Cooper guessed.

Slowly, the old hermit turned around to face his visitors, trembling a little. "I'll tell you what I'm afraid of." He took a deep breath. "Bergens!"

Aha! Biggie thought. *So that's it! Herman's afraid of Bergens! He doesn't know that the Bergens don't eat us anymore. That we've made friends with them. As long as he doesn't find that out, maybe we'll be able to scare—*

"Oh, you don't need to be afraid of Bergens anymore!" Cooper said cheerfully. "They're our frie—"

Before Cooper could finish his sentence, Biggie and Guy clamped their hands over his mouth. He kept talking, but his speech was muffled.

"Mmmph-mmm-nnmph-mnnh!"

Herman squinted at them suspiciously. "What was he saying about not having to be afraid of Bergens anymore? Why would that be? Did they all shrink down to the size of my pinkie finger? That'd be great, because then I could stomp on 'em!" He stomped his feet on the ground, taking great joy in pretending to squish Bergens. "Hee, hee, hee!"

Biggie hesitated. If Bergens were the one thing they knew Herman was afraid of, it seemed like a bad idea to tell him they weren't scary anymore. How would they ever frighten him into remembering "The Dancemaster's Song"? On the other hand, it didn't seem very nice to lie to an old hermit who might be helping them.

"Cooper's right," Biggie admitted. "Bergens are our friends now."

"Since when?" Herman asked, amazed.

"Since Poppy showed them they had the power inside themselves to be happy," Guy explained. "They didn't need to eat us to experience true happiness. Didn't you hear about that?"

"I don't get out much," Herman said drily.

He pointed to his chest with a thumb. "Hermit, remember?"

Biggie let Cooper go. "Well, it's all true!" Cooper blurted out. "There's no reason to be scared of Bergens anymore. They're our great big pals!"

Herman looked extremely doubtful. "I don't believe it. To me, Bergens are still the most terrifying things around!" He shuddered.

And that shudder gave Biggie an idea. . . .

CHAPTER NINE

"Well, thanks anyway, Herman," Biggie said. "It sure was nice meeting you. C'mon, guys, let's go."

He turned and rushed across the bumpy root, heading back toward Troll Village. Guy and Cooper hurried after him. They were surprised that Biggie was leaving so suddenly. So was Herman.

"Um, okay," the hermit said, puzzled. "Thanks for the Sweetbug Sticky Sap!"

Cooper and Guy caught up with Biggie just as he emerged from the twisted roots of the gigantic tree. He started running toward the village.

"Hey, Biggie!" Cooper called. "Wait up!"

"Yeah," Guy said. "Why did you leave so suddenly? Herman hasn't remembered the song yet! I was still trying to think of other ways to scare him!"

Biggie paused long enough to turn around and explain his idea. "Herman's afraid of Bergens, right?" The other two nodded.

"Oh, I know!" Cooper said. "We're going to stand on each other's shoulders and disguise ourselves as a Bergen! Brilliant idea, Biggie!"

"We could do that," Biggie said. "Or we could just get a *real* Bergen to help us!"

"Where are we going to get a real Bergen?" Guy asked. "It's a long way to Bergen Town, and the big dance will be here soon."

"Don't you remember?" Biggie said. "Bridget's visiting Poppy today! If we hurry, we can still catch her!"

He turned and resumed running toward Poppy's pod, scanning the village for Bridget. In Troll Village, a Bergen would be very easy to spot.

But he didn't see her.

When he reached Poppy's home, he panted, "Poppy! Where's Bridget?"

Poppy came out the door, surprised to see Biggie out of breath. Guy and Cooper ran up behind him, breathing just as hard.

"She just left!" Poppy said. "She's headed

back to Bergen Town, but if you hurry, you should be able to catch her."

lllllllll

Biggie, Cooper, and Guy ran in the direction Poppy was pointing. They whipped their hair around branches and swung through the trees. They hadn't gone far into the forest when they heard Bridget ahead of them, whistling a cheerful tune.

"BRIDGET! WAIT! STOP!" the three Trolls shouted at the tops of their lungs.

It wasn't always easy for Bergens to hear Troll voices. Luckily, Bridget had excellent hearing. She paused and cocked her head. *I hear little voices. Is someone calling me?* she thought.

Guy caught up to her first. Standing at her

feet, he waved his arms frantically. "Bridget! Down here!"

Bridget looked down and saw the three Trolls. She smiled and bent over, putting her friendly face close to theirs.

"Hello there!" she said. "What's up? Did I leave something at Poppy's?"

Biggie shook his head. "No, you didn't leave anything—at least, not as far as I know. We just wondered if you might have time before you head home to do us a quick favor."

"A favor?" Bridget looked intrigued.

ℓℓℓℓℓℓℓℓℓ

In his cave under the tree, Herman spread a thick layer of Sweetbug Sticky Sap on another piece of toast. Just as he was about to take a big bite, he heard a familiar voice outside.

"Oh, Herman! Could you come out here for a minute, please?"

He recognized the voice. It was one of those Trolls who'd visited earlier—the big blue one. He sighed and put the piece of toast back on his chipped plate. Then he headed out through the narrow passage between the rocks to see what the big blue Troll wanted this time.

"What is it?" he growled as he stepped out from the rocks.

He found himself face to face with . . . a Bergen!

"ROOWWWWRRRR!" growled Bridget.

"YAAAAAHHH!" screamed Herman in shock and terror, his long hair standing straight up. He clutched the sides of his head and fell to his knees, trembling. "A Bergen! A Bergen!

Please don't eat me! Please don't eat me!"

Bridget looked apologetic. "Oh! I'm not going to eat you! I'm sorry I scared you! Have a nice day!"

She withdrew her head from the ancient tree's tangled roots and stood. Biggie waved up to her. "Thanks, Bridget!" he called.

"No problem!" she said. "Good luck!" She tromped off into the woods, heading back toward Bergen Town.

Biggie, Guy, and Cooper helped Herman to his feet.

"It's okay, Herman," Biggie said soothingly. "She's our friend! All the Bergens are now, remember?"

"A Bergen," Herman muttered, still shocked. "Right here at my doorstep!"

"Did you remember?" Guy asked eagerly.

The old hermit looked puzzled. "Remember what?"

"The song!" Cooper said. "The magic song that makes you a dancer!"

Herman just stood there a moment, his eyes moving back and forth. Then he breathed in through his nose, opened his mouth, and started to sing. . . .

CHAPTER TEN

The old hermit's voice was a little creaky, but the words he sang were easy to make out:

If you want to learn some tricky new dance,
Just warble this wonderful song.
You'll get those difficult moves at a glance
And you never will go wrong!
The secret is knowing you know the dance
Deep inside your heart.

Just give your dancing feet a chance.

You'll get it from the start!

Steppity, steppity, steppity-step.

So easy for you now.

Yessiree, yessir, oh, yeppity-yep.

The dancers will all say "Wow!"

No matter what musical tune they play

On fiddle or flute or gong,

You'll master each dance in a magical way

By singing the Dancemaster's Song!

By singing . . . THE DANCEMASTER'S SONG!

As he sang, Herman's voice became stronger and more confident. He gestured for Biggie to join in. At first, Biggie wasn't sure of the words, but after they'd sung the song together several times, Biggie knew all the verses by heart. Herman was so delighted with himself for remembering the ancient song that he broke into a little jig. Biggie joined him, matching his steps perfectly—with no trouble at all!

"Look at Biggie dance!" Cooper said, amazed. "The song works!"

"Well," Guy said, not completely convinced, "Herman's jig is pretty simple. We'll have to see how Biggie does with *our* dance."

"Then let's hurry!" Cooper insisted. He called to Biggie, who was still singing the song over and over with Herman. "Come on, Biggie! Let's go! When we get back to Guy's dance studio, you can test your new skills!"

Biggie stopped singing and nodded. Then he turned to Herman. "Thank you so much! How can I ever repay you?" He opened his arms wide and leaned over to hug the hermit, but Herman stopped him.

"Not with a hug! That's for sure!" he growled. Then his voice softened. "But if you ever feel like bringing me another jar of Sweetbug Sticky Sap . . ."

"You got it!" Biggie said, grinning.

"Next time bring a BIG jar!" Herman said.

lllllllll

The three dancers hurried back through Troll Village to Guy's studio. The whole way, Biggie quietly sang the magical song to himself, afraid he'd forget it. *"Steppity, steppity, steppity-step! So easy for you now. . . ."*

"Yippity, yoppity, yoopity-yup . . . ," Cooper sang happily.

"Um, Cooper!" Biggie cried. "Would you mind not making up new words, please? I'm afraid I'll forget the right ones, and then the song won't work."

"Oops," Cooper said. "Sorry."

"That's okay," Biggie reassured his friend. "Maybe just let me sing the song by myself so I can be sure to remember it."

"You got it!" Cooper said. "I'll be quiet as a Speckbug!" But before he'd gone two steps, he was absentmindedly singing to himself, *"Blippity, bloppity, bloopity-blorp . . ."*

Sighing, Biggie stuck his fingers in his ears and kept singing as they used their hair to rapidly swing through the village.

In his dance studio, Guy was ready to start

the music. "Okay," he said. "Here goes. The moment of truth! Ready, Biggie?"

Biggie was still quietly singing "The Dancemaster's Song" to himself, but now he stopped. *Am I ready?* he wondered. *Will the song work? Or am I just going to stumble around and make a fool of myself again? I don't think I could bear that. . . .*

He gave Guy a little nod. Guy tapped the Tunebug, and DJ Suki's high-speed song blasted out into the studio. "A-five, six, seven, eight . . . ," Guy counted, cuing Cooper to start with him.

Cooper and Guy broke into the fast dance, moving their arms and feet in unison. They kicked, spun, jumped, and whirled. And then . . .

Biggie was dancing with them! He stepped

in between them and started matching their moves! The three Trolls danced in perfect step to the music. Biggie didn't miss a beat!

When the music stopped, they fell into each other's arms, laughing and cheering. The magical song worked!

"Perfect!" Guy said. "But just to be sure, let's do it again!" He tapped the bug, and the music started over. They danced the entire routine, and Biggie didn't make a single mistake!

"WHOO-HOO!" Cooper cheered. Biggie had a huge smile on his face. A tear slipped down his cheek, but it was a happy tear.

"Okay," Guy said. "That's great. Now let's work on our solo dances—our signature moves." They found places in the dance where one Troll could go into the center and do his own special move while the other two kept dancing the set routine. Cooper did his flashiest four-legged, long-necked steps. Guy sent glitter flying into the air. And Biggie swayed to the music.

As they watched themselves in the mirrors, they felt proud. Their dance really was good!

"This is going to look even better once we're wearing our new outfits!" Cooper exclaimed.

New outfits? Biggie thought. *I forgot all about the matching outfits Satin and Chenille are making for us. Am I going to look ridiculous wearing such a flashy costume?*

"Do you think our outfits will make it hard to do any of these dance moves?" Biggie worried.

Guy grinned. "There's only one way to find out!"

"You've come . . . ," Satin began.

". . . just in time!" Chenille finished.

The twins explained that they'd just finished making the outfits for Guy, Cooper, and Biggie, and they'd love to have their friends try them on.

"You can use our dressing rooms . . . ," Chenille started.

". . . if you'd like," Satin completed.

"No need!" Guy said. Since he wasn't wearing anything except glitter, he pulled his new outfit on right there in front of the others. Cooper and Biggie took theirs into the dressing rooms.

Biggie hung his outfit up and examined it. Though it was made with much flashier material than he was used to, with sequins and sparkles, the basic design was actually very similar to his usual shorts and vest. When he put the pieces on, they fit perfectly!

He stepped out of the dressing room.

"Ooh!" Satin and Chenille said together. "Perfect!"

"How does it feel?" Satin asked, looking him up and down.

"Very comfortable," Biggie reported.

"Good," Satin said. "Comfort's important!"

"Especially when you're dancing!" Chenille agreed.

When the three dancers stood together, they saw that the outfits matched, but each one was personalized. Cooper's included a sparkly hat shaped like his usual green one—with a small feather added. Biggie's resembled his daily

wear, but in glistening material. And Guy's showed off as much of his glittery self as possible.

"Fantastic!" Cooper cheered.

"So sparkly!" Guy added.

"They're wonderful," Biggie said, tearing up a little. "Thank you so much!"

"It's completely and utterly . . . ," Satin began.

". . . our pleasure!" Chenille finished. "We can't wait to see you dance in them!"

CHAPTER ELEVEN

The next morning, the day of the big dance, Biggie baked plenty of cupcakes and cookies, just as he'd promised Poppy he would. While he spread frosting and scattered sprinkles, he quietly sang "The Dancemaster's Song" over and over. *"The secret is knowing you know the dance deep inside your heart. . . . "*

"Mew?" Mr. Dinkles asked.

"This song?" Biggie said as he packed

cookies into baskets. "It's a magical song! It helped me learn a really tricky dance!"

"Mew," Mr. Dinkles said.

"It is NOT annoying!" Biggie argued. "It's . . . extremely useful! Watch this!"

Biggie did a little section of the dance—and came very close to knocking a basket full of cupcakes onto the floor.

"Mew!" Mr. Dinkles cried.

"Don't worry," Biggie said, pushing the basket back on the shelf. "I'll be careful. Oh, by the way, Satin and Chenille made you something for tonight!"

Biggie went into the back room and returned with a new outfit for Mr. Dinkles. It matched Biggie's perfectly!

"Mew!" Mr. Dinkles said, gawking.

Biggie smiled. "I'm glad you like it!" For the first time, he was feeling excited for the dance.

lllllllll

That evening, Guy and Cooper stopped by the bakery to help Biggie carry his cookies and cupcakes to the dance. They had their new outfits with them.

"Shouldn't we change into our outfits before we go to the dance?" Biggie asked.

"No way!" Cooper said. "That would spoil our entrance! We have to change into our new threads backstage, just before we go out to perform."

"Then when everybody sees what we're wearing," Guy said, "they'll all be like 'Wow! Check THEM out!'"

"Yeah," Cooper said, grinning, "they'll all

be like 'Wow! Guy Diamond's WEARING CLOTHES!'"

They laughed. Then they picked up the baskets full of sweets and headed out. Biggie carried Mr. Dinkles in his arms.

ℓℓℓℓℓℓℓℓℓℓ

The village square was lit up by twinkling Glowflies and Sparkbugs. DJ Suki had some music going—a little softer and slower than the dance track she'd put together for Guy, Cooper, and Biggie. Night-blooming flowers opened and scented the evening air.

It was magical.

Every Troll in the village had gathered for the big dance. They were all laughing and enjoying themselves. As soon as Biggie and his dance partners arrived with the freshly baked cupcakes and cookies, eager hands plunged into the baskets. Seconds later, crumbs were flying, and more than one Troll had a frosting mustache.

"Welcome, everyone!" Poppy called from the front of the big stage. She was wearing a lovely new blue dress with a matching hairband. "I hope you're all ready to dance!"

Everyone cheered and clapped.

"Okay, then," Poppy said, grinning. "LET'S DANCE!"

Thumping music kicked in, and the Trolls started to move. One by one, groups of dancers made their way to the stage, eager to perform the routines they'd prepared.

From the back of the crowd, Biggie watched the other dancers nervously, still quietly singing

"The Dancemaster's Song" to himself. *"Just give your dancing feet a chance. You'll get it from the start!"*

First up were Smidge and Fuzzbert. They danced around the whole stage, circling each other, facing the crowd. Then they turned and faced each other from opposite ends of the stage. Smidge clapped her hands, and Fuzzbert sprinted straight toward her!

Just when everyone thought he was going to slam into her, Fuzzbert jumped into the air . . . and Smidge caught him with her hair! She lifted him high overhead with ease, the same way she lifted weights every morning. Fuzzbert grunted and mumbled with delight.

"HRNT GRURNK HARN GRARRRN!"

Smidge danced all around the stage, lifting

and lowering Fuzzbert. She finally set him down, and they both took deep bows. Everyone cheered!

"See?" Guy whispered to Biggie. "Very supportive crowd! Nothing to worry about!"

"Right," Biggie said uncertainly. "Nothing."

Next up were Harper, Maddy, and Karma. The music shifted. At first, they all did the same steps together. And they were good, moving and kicking with ease and grace. Then they started to do unique moves that showed off their special skills. Karma, who loved nature, held up her hands and coaxed two Critterbugs to fly down and land on her shoulders, making it look as though she had wings. Maddy danced while styling her two partners' hair, her feet never missing a beat. And Harper, the village's finest artist, quickly dashed off a beautiful painting of the three girls dancing together, finishing it just before the music ended.

As the performers bowed, the crowd went wild!

"Soon it'll be our turn!" Cooper said excitedly. "I can't WAIT to get up there! Can you, Biggie?"

"Oh, no," Biggie said unconvincingly. "Can't wait."

"Well, you won't have to wait long!" Guy said. "We're up after the twins! Come on—let's go change into our outfits!"

As they headed backstage, Biggie felt as though a huge flock of Colorflies had moved in to his stomach. He hugged Mr. Dinkles so tightly, the pet worm squeaked in complaint.

"Mew!"

"Oh, sorry!" Biggie said, loosening his embrace. "By the way, you look GREAT in your new outfit!"

"Mew mew," Mr. Dinkles said proudly.

When Satin and Chenille hit the stage, they looked fabulous in their brand-new costumes. Some Trolls in the crowd thought their connected hair might limit their dancing, but it turned out to be a terrific advantage. They used it to spin, flip, and whirl each other across the stage, taking turns keeping their feet on the ground and flying through the air. Their dance was dazzling!

Backstage, Biggie finished putting on the costume the twins had made for him. He heard the audience cheering for their dance.

"Wish me luck!" he said to Mr. Dinkles as he

set him down in a comfortable spot.

"Mew!" Mr. Dinkles said.

Then Poppy announced them.

"And now, get ready for the unique dance stylings of Guy Diamond, Cooper, and Biggie!" The audience applauded.

The three dancers hurried out onto the stage. Spotlights hit them. In the brightness, Biggie couldn't even see the Trolls out in the crowd. But he could *feel* all those eyes staring at him. His heart was pounding.

"Oh my gah," Smidge said in her loud deep voice. "Guy Diamond is wearing CLOTHES!"

"Told you," Cooper whispered to his two dancemates, giggling.

DJ Suki hit the music. It was the fastest song of the night so far.

But suddenly, everything seemed to slow down for Biggie. He tried to remember the first step in their dance routine . . . and couldn't think of it! HE'D FORGOTTEN THE WHOLE ROUTINE!

Then he heard the magical song playing in his head: *"The secret is knowing you know the dance deep inside your heart. Just give your dancing feet a chance. You'll get it from the start!"*

His feet started moving. He remembered the routine! He, Guy, and Cooper were moving in perfect unison, matching steps exactly! When it came time for Biggie's special move, he shifted into the middle and swayed back and forth in time to the music. Then he went right back into the group dance, never missing a step.

Before he knew it, the dance was over. He'd done it perfectly! Not a single mistake! He'd even had *fun* doing it! The audience roared, clapped, and stomped their feet as the three dancers held their final poses, smiling huge.

Then, out of the corner of his eye, Biggie noticed something.

At the edge of the crowd, all by himself, Herman was applauding and cheering. When Biggie caught his eye, the old hermit waved and winked.

And after Biggie left the stage, the hermit let him hug him!

"Okay, okay," Herman said, finally pulling free. "Now you REALLY owe me another jar of Sweetbug Sticky Sap!"